ALSO BY STAN LEE

Origins of Marvel Comics
Son of Origins
Bring on the Bad Guys
Superhero Women
How to Draw Comics the Marvel Way
The Incredible Hulk
The Silver Surfer
The Mightly World of Marvel Pin-Up Book
Marvel's Greatest Superhero Battles
The Amazing Spider-Man
The Mightly Marvel Jumbo Fun Book

Dr. Strange

by

STAN LEE

A FIRESIDE BOOK
Published by
SIMON AND SCHUSTER • New York

Copyright © 1979 by Marvel Comics Group,
A Division of Cadence Industries Corporation
All rights reserved
including the right of reproduction
in whole or in part in any form
A Fireside Book
Published by Simon and Schuster
A Division of Gulf & Western Corporation
Simon & Schuster Building
Rockefeller Center
1230 Avenue of the Americas
New York, New York 10020

Manufactured in the United States of America
1   2   3   4   5   6   7   8   9   10
1   2   3   4   5   6   7   8   9   10 pbk.

Library of Congress Cataloging in Publication Data

Lee, Stan.
  Dr. Strange

  (A Fireside book)
  1. Doctor Strange (Comic strip) I. Title.
PN6728.D58L4   741.5'973   79-17028

ISBN 0-671-24814-6 pbk.
    0-671-25206-2

DEDICATION

Dedicated to Steve Ditko, who gave such fabulous form, substance, and style to our Master of the Mystic Arts when Stephen Strange was just a'borning, and who set the mood for an aura of exotic enchantment destined to thrill generations of readers for decades to come

Dedicated also to Phil De Guere, who, almost twenty years later, had both the faith and the rare ability to take our creation of Dr. Strange and translate it with such sincerity and talent into a brilliant, unforgettable television experience.

PREFACE

Dr. Strange has always had a very special place in my warm and loving heart. Sure, I'm proud of Spider-Man, the Incredible Hulk, the Fantastic Four, the Silver Surfer, Mighty Thor, and all the rest of the multi-muscled merrymakers in our little Marvel menagerie. I love them all. But good ol' Doc is different. Let me tell you why.

The one element that sets superhero characters apart from the average, normal, everyday type of fictional good guy is the element of fantasy. Superheroes are different. Especially Marvel superheroes. You know what I mean. Our costumed cavorters aren't exactly the type of cutups you'll find lounging around in your neighborhood bowling alley—or starring in an average TV cops-and-robbers show. They're one of a kind. They're unique. They're different. That's why readers dig 'em. That's why I dig them. And that's why I dig Dr. Strange. Even in a whacky world of swingin' superheroes, you've got to admit our magician is different.

One of the differences I've always liked most about our sagacious sorcerer is the way he speaks. After all, how many guys do you know who can—with a straight face—make casual allusions to the "Hoary Hosts of Hoggoth," or the "Shades of the Shadowy Seraphim," or even, if you will, the "Crimson Bands of Cytorrak"? As a matter of fact, since I'm unabashedly corny in my admitted affection for high-flown, flowery, pseudo-Shakespearean and quasi-biblical dialog, I've always gotten the biggest kick out of writing the valiant verbiage for Dr. Strange, Thor, and the Silver Surfer—as well as Galactus, Odin, Dr. Doom, and Mephisto. You just can't have those kinda cats rapping away like you and I might do! But, it's Dr. Strange alone who has to recite his spooky spells and indecipherable incantations—and I sure do love to write those nutty things.

And how about those pandemonious plots!

How can you not have a special spot in your heart for a fella who's as apt to visit the Dark Dimension—or the Nightmare World—or the realm of the Dread Dormammu, as he is to drop in at the neighborhood supermarket for a bag of Fritos? I mean—man, when you pick up a Dr. Strange to read, you know you're not gonna get "Dick and Jane went up the hill"!

Okay. So what will you get? Well, since you bothered to ask . . .

In this brain-blasting book alone, you'll be running into (and oh, how I envy you!) the merciless, murderous Baron Mordo; the aged, anguished, ever-adorable Ancient One; the naughty, nasty, necromantic known as Nightmare; Aggamon, ruthless ruler of the Purple Dimension; a huge and hideous house that lives; a trap of horror on the other side of the world; the fascinating though ill-fated female known as Clea; the sinister sorceress called Shazana; the wondrous and deadly Wand of Watoomb; and the usual agonized assortment of courageous cops, craven crooks, and countless other cuddly, incidental characters.

Hey, but that isn't all! We've also got some great and ginchy guest stars like Spider-Man, Loki, and the Mighty Thor—not to mention such titanic tableaus as the time Doc Strange appears as the main guest on a national network prime-time TV special—or the senses-shattering scenes wherein our hero dares to unleash the almost unmentionable spells of the omnipotent Oshtur! Yep, I think we've got a surprise or two in store for you.

But, before we get started, have you ever wondered why the mystic arts seem to hold such far-reaching fascination for the reading public? Why is it that the subject of magic and the shadowy realm of sorcery have captured and intrigued the minds of men since time immemorial? (Or even since time memorial, as well, if you insist on splitting hairs.) I don't claim to have the ultimate and absolute answer, but I'll give you my opinion anyway—especially since there's no way you can shut me up, and I love a captive audience.

It isn't the act of magic per se that turns people on. Uh uh. It's what that mystical feat represents. Magic represents a regimen, a series of laws that go beyond the natural sciences as we know and understand them. In point of fact, magic represents the theory that the supernatural really exists—and that's what this is all about.

Everyone wants to believe in the supernatural. Everyone wants to believe there's much more to the world than what we can see, and feel, and taste. Everyone wants to believe that somewhere out there, beyond the reach of our own mortal knowledge, beyond the stretch and scope of our imagination, is another universe: A greater, vaster, far more wondrous universe—a universe, or a utopia, or a heaven, call it what you will—a dream, perhaps, that all of us share, a dream that may link us with some sort of immortality.

And so we turn to the lore of magic. There, we seek hints, and clues, and dimly glimpsed traces of the miraculous world that we so avidly wish for. For only there, in the wild, unfettered domain of all that is mystical, might we one day find the secret of the supernatural—the secret that man has sought since first he walked upon the good, green earth and marveled at the mystery of the heavens.

Whew! I didn't mean to get so heavy, or to wax so flowery about the subject. I guess what I'm really trying to say is that we all realize there must be more to life than this. There must be more to the sum total of human existence than that which meets the eye. Okay, so how do we find it? One way is by trying to free our imagination, trying to grasp the concepts that have eluded us for ages. And how do we do it? Aha! You guessed it: by telling, and reading, and studying, and sharing the stories and legends that seek to open the doorways of our minds—that seek to strip bare the secrets of the world of magic.

Of course, there's also something else. Reading stories of sorcery and the enchantment of other worlds is simply downright fun! Anyone with half an imagination is bound to get a kick out of tales that present characters and situations wilder and weirder than any we have ever known. Who among us can resist the lure of stories that feature mystery, fantasy, action, menace, and magic, all tied together tidily and threateningly by their incredible link to the world of the supernatural? Forget the philosophy, forget all my high-flown, windy theories, forget the sociological and psychological symbolism. Just remember the most important point of all—everyone enjoys a juicy tale of mystery and magic—and that's where Dr. Strange is at!

Incidentally, lots of people have asked where I dug up all the strange-sounding names with which our tales are so generously sprinkled. People have theorized that they bear the influence of ancient Druid writings, or that they come from research into the genealogy of Tibetan lamas, or that I just plain copied the hieroglyphics from Egyptian pyramids. Well, even though I really hate to destroy such glamorous and erudite theories, I must honestly admit that they aren't consciously based on anything. I just thunk 'em up. It's one of the things I get the biggest kick out of—inventing nutty names.

Take Dormammu, for instance. My biggest problem was trying to decide whether it should have two *r*'s or two *m*'s. And then, after writing it both ways and deciding I preferred the double *m*, I was faced with the critical choice of whether the first *m* or the second *m* should be the one to be doubled. So, I wrote "Dormmamu." I looked at it. I pronounced it. I felt it wasn't right. Then I wrote "Dormammu." Wow! It's like the difference between night and day. Look at it. It speaks volumes. It doesn't just lie there—it seems charged with energy! What's that you say? You can't see the difference? And you don't care one way or the other? Well then, would you like to discuss "Hoggoth"? Aw, forget it. We'll save that for Volume Two.

You've got to forgive me. I suppose I should be a lot more serious about all of this. After all, here I am writing a book that will doubtless be on the best-seller list for years and years. (I've got this friend, you see, named Bernie Best-Seller, and he writes these little lists. Skip it. It's a private joke!) The thing is, it's really hard for me to be very serious about anything for very long.

But you're not grasping this exemplary edition in your greedy little hands because you want me to tell you all about my personality problems. At least I hope not.

So, let's stop dawdling and get to the matter at hand. The time is come to dim the lights, settle back in your favorite chair, and prepare to cross the mysterious threshold that separates the world we inhabit from the indescribable realm of the mystic arts. And remember, I'm as nervous as you are. But we needn't be afraid. I vow by the Roving Rings of Raggadorr—Dr. Strange will see us through!

Excelsior

Stan Lee

Stan Lee
Beverly Hills 1979

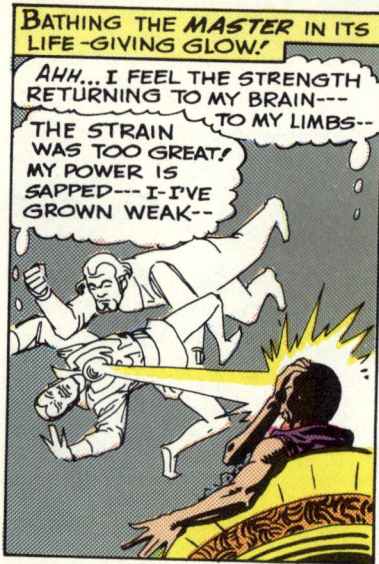

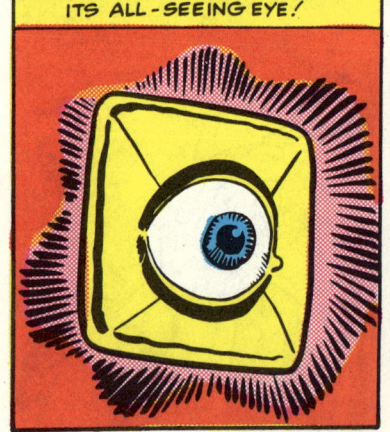

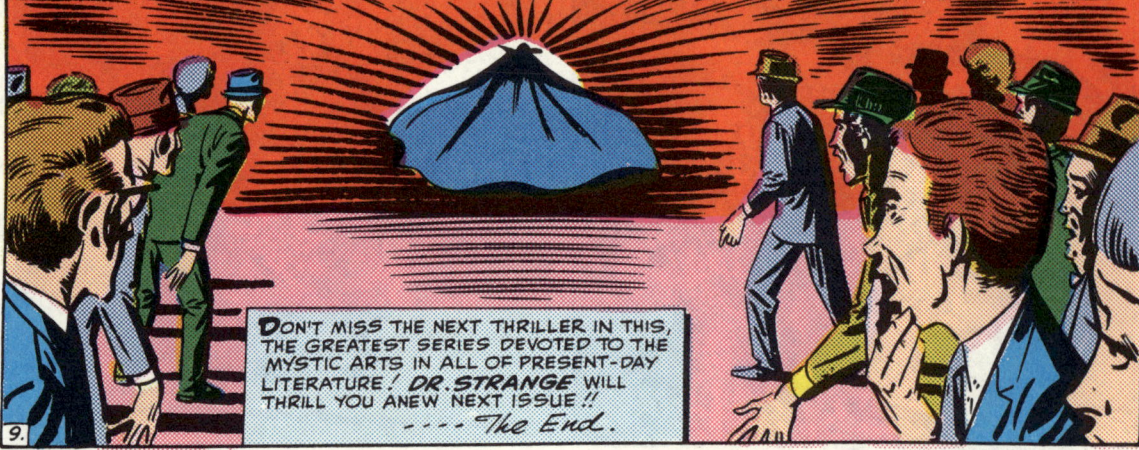

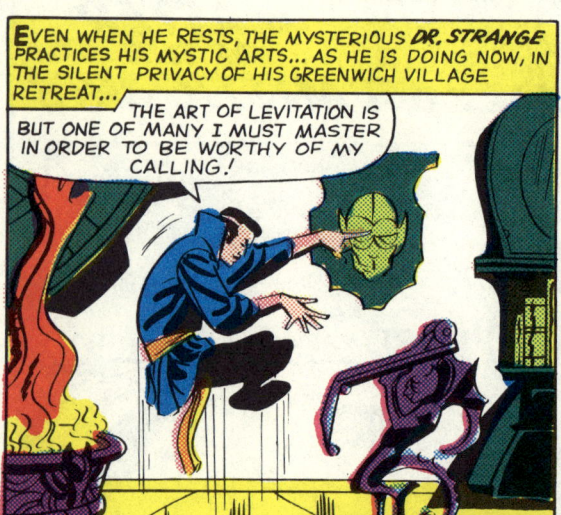
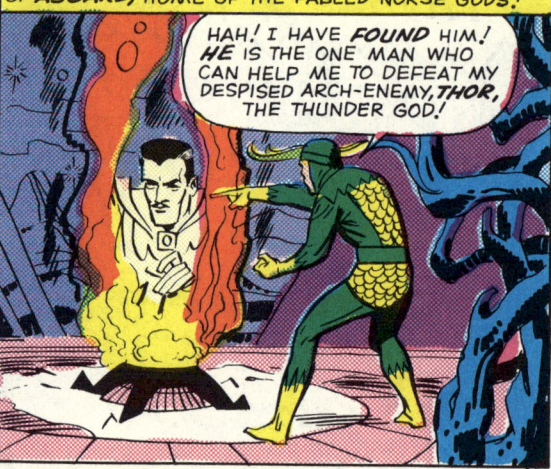

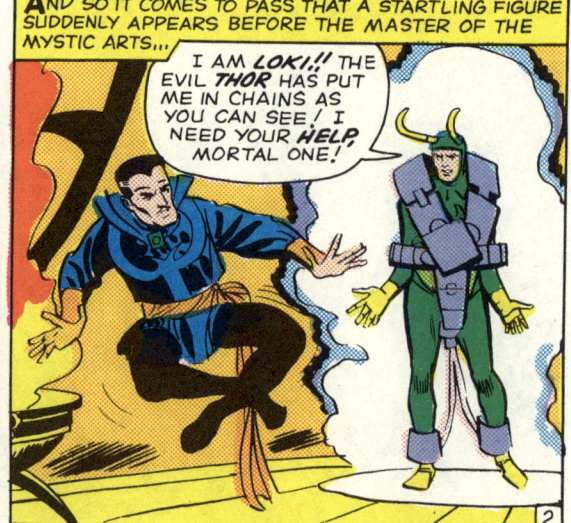

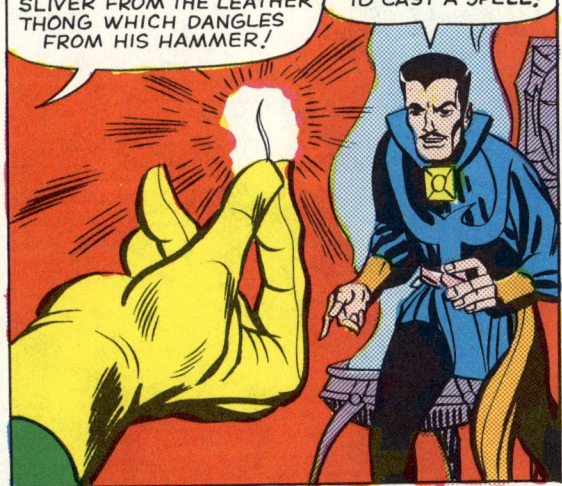

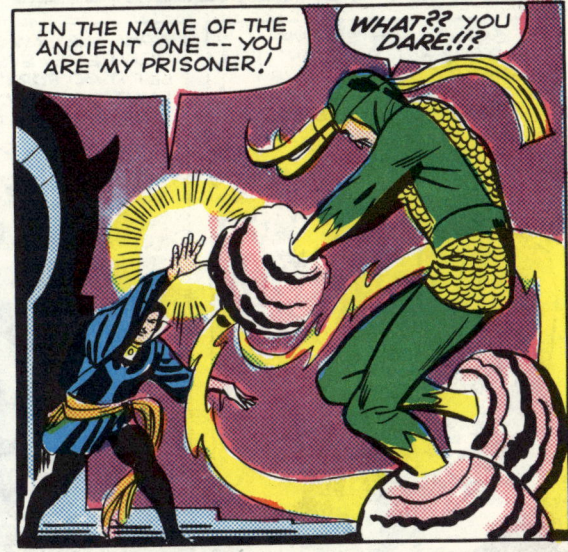

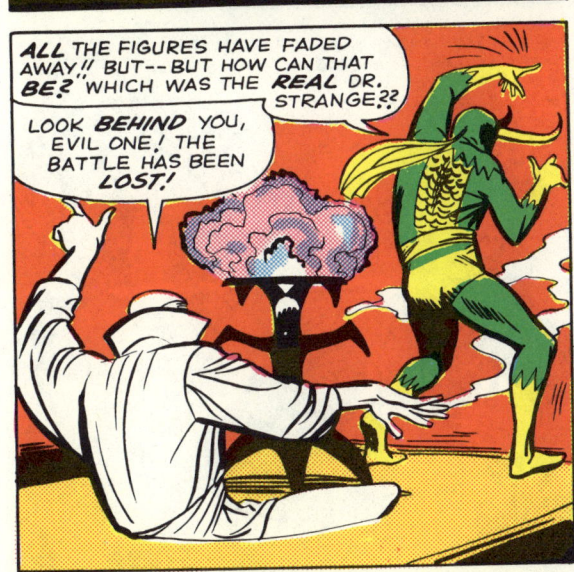

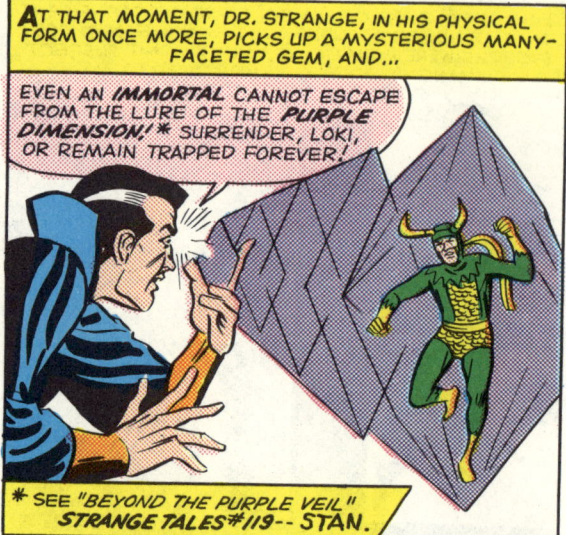

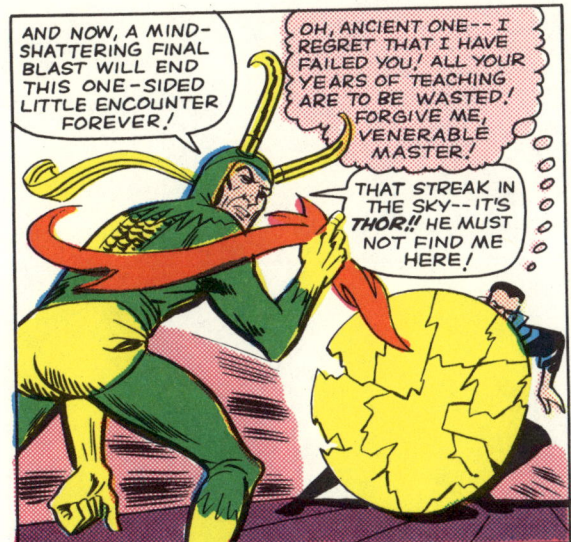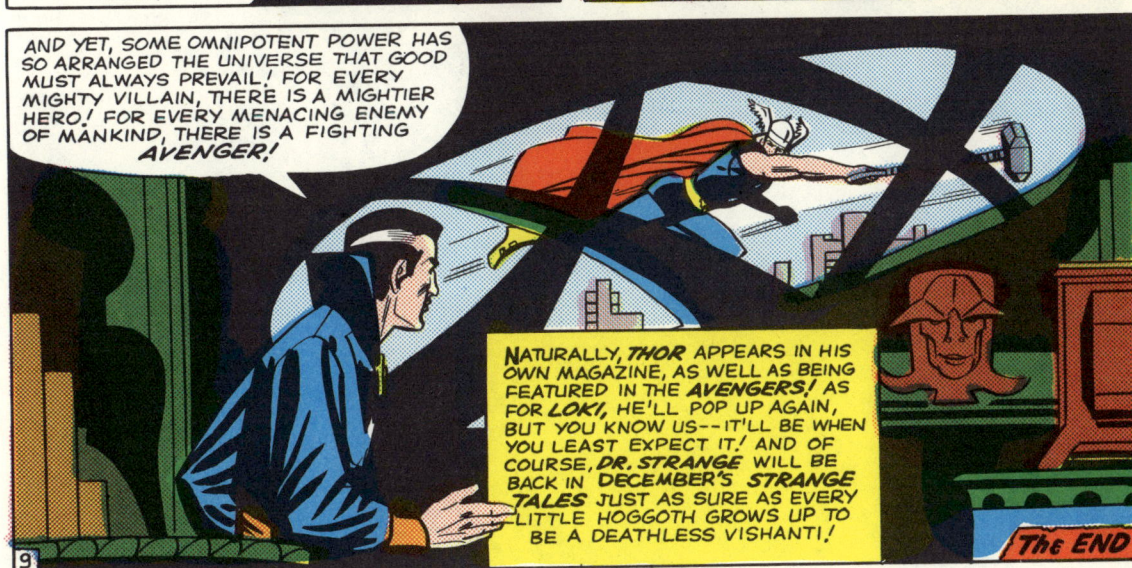

See? Didn't I tell you not to worry? Us good guys always win.

But now, it's time for one of our most famous trilogies. We start with "The Hunter and the Hunted," segue immediately into "Face to Face with Baron Mordo," and then leave you shouting for more as we wrap it up with "A Nameless Land, a Timeless Time"—one of my all-time favorite titles. After all, if the boob tube can feature never-ending mini-series, surely mighty Marvel can do no less. Hey, we practically invented the things!

Y'know, one of the reasons I've always been fond of Baron Mordo—as a villainous character, I mean—is the fact that his power is so close to that which Dr. Strange possesses. When you have to spend a lot of time writing these stirring little sagas, it makes it really interesting to dream up traps and tricks and tantalizing little tests of strength and shrewdness for two antagonists who are very nearly evenly matched.

Another thing that makes mean ol' Mordo such a practically perfect villain is the fact that, unlike many of our other bombastic baddies, his baronship possesses not one single, solitary, worthwhile or redeeming trait that anyone can find. He's really one baaaad dude! He'd probably not only take candy from a baby but also sell it back to the poor kid at twice the price! In fact, Mordo's so totally rotten, he makes Dr. Doom seem like a compulsive altruist!

Anyhow, the three modern masterpieces of mystical mayhem that you will soon read and rave about start off in the mysterious city of Hong Kong. How Doc got there, or why, I can't quite remember, but I'm sure he must have had a reason—and if that satisfies me, then it oughta be good enough for you too! Actually, I do recall that Stephen was trying to save the venerable Ancient One by making Mordo and his murderous minions pursue our hero, to take the heat off the Ancient One himself.

Hey, I just had a sensational idea. Can you imagine what a kick it would be if the Ancient One met Spider-Man's Aunt May and the two of 'em hit it off? They'd be the biggest item since Romeo and Juliet! See? That's what happens whenever I'm trying to be serious. All of a sudden some nutty thought gives me a zap—and then it won't let go. Can you imagine Dormammu as the best man and Shazana as a bridesmaid? By the Eternal Eye of Agamotto, it's just too much!

Okay, that's enough of my undisciplined stream of consciousness. If you've read this illuminating intro thus far, you've earned yourself the right to a little enjoyment now! So, let's temporarily tear away from each other again—difficult though it may be—and see what's goin' down out there on the other side of the planet as dauntless Doc battles to save himself from the world's most magical assassination!

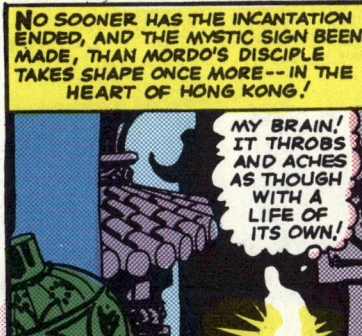

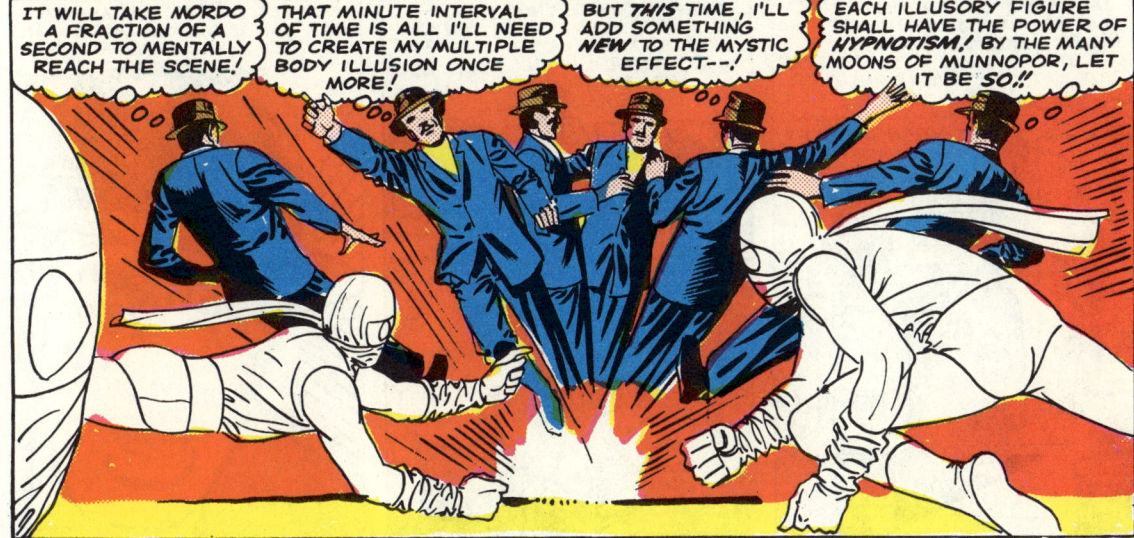

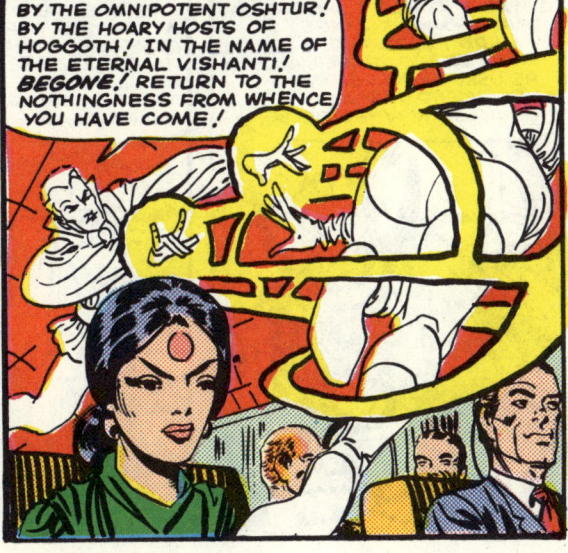

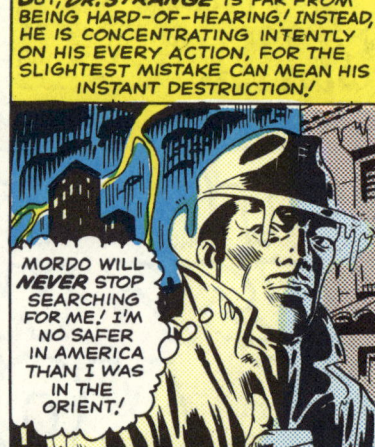

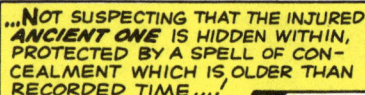

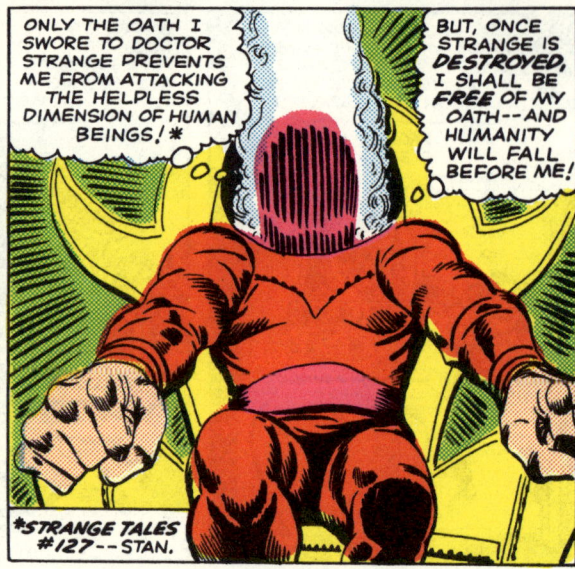

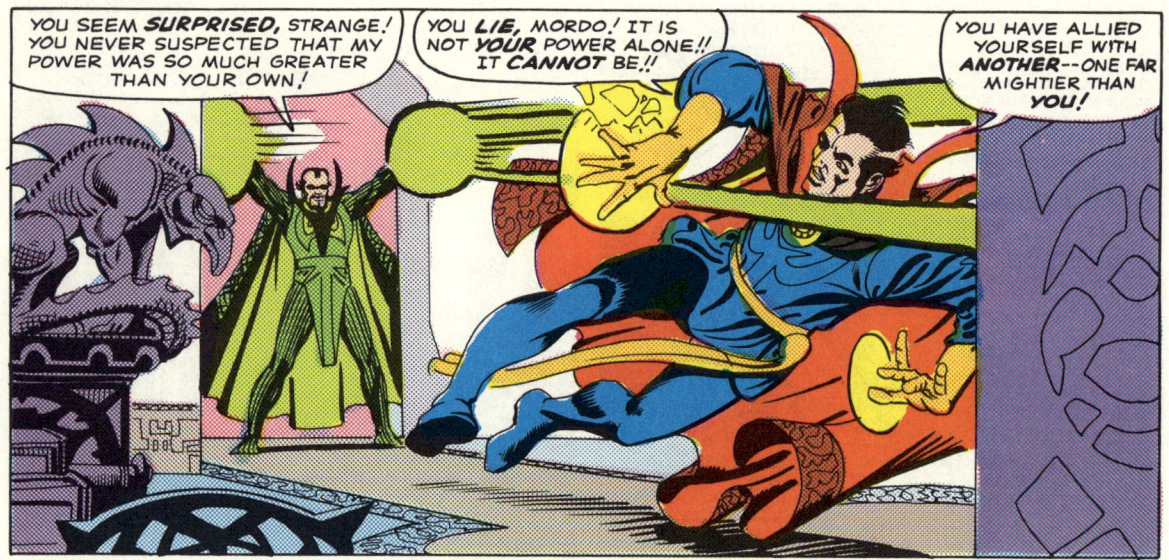

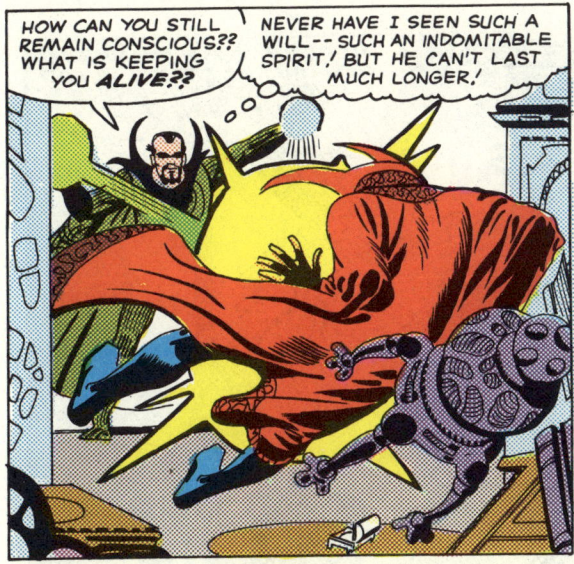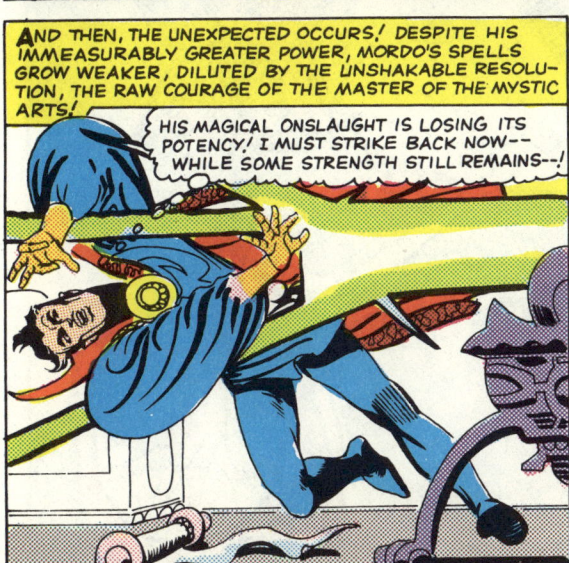

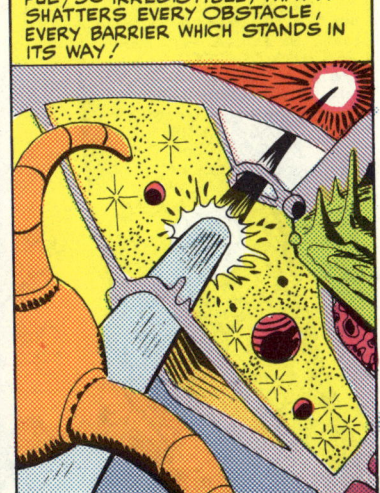

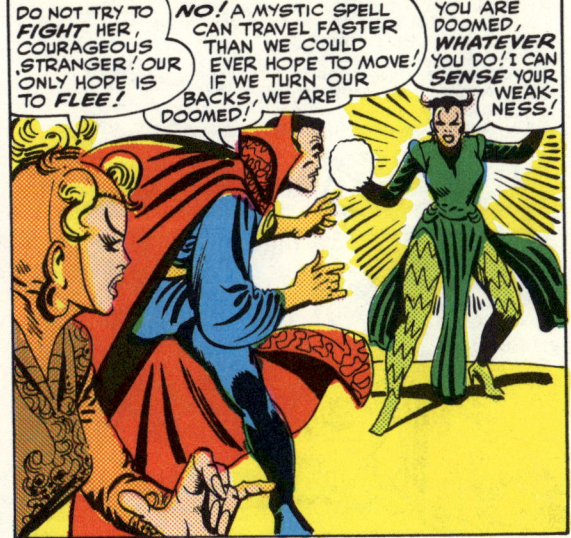

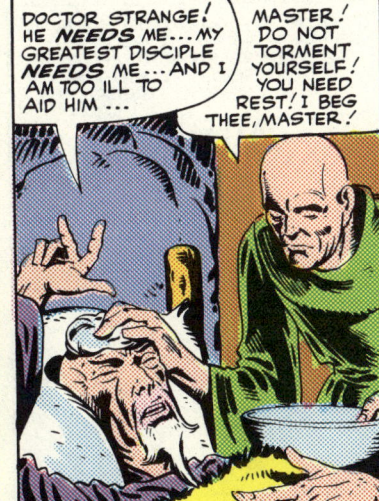

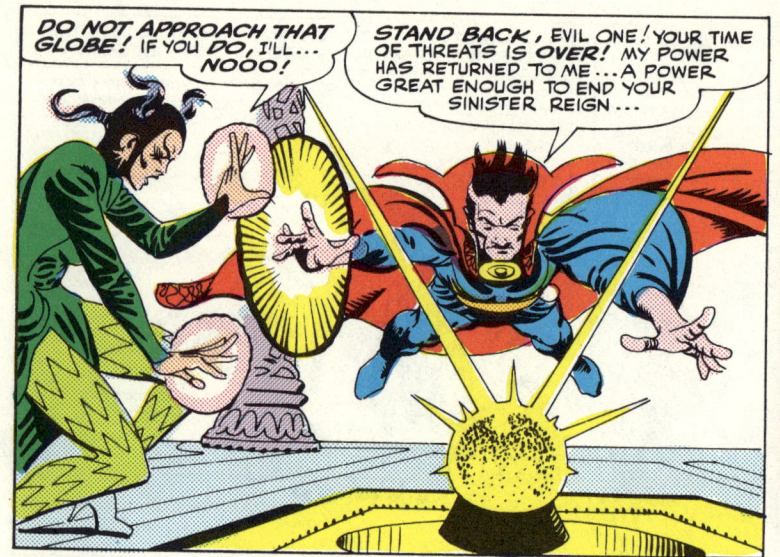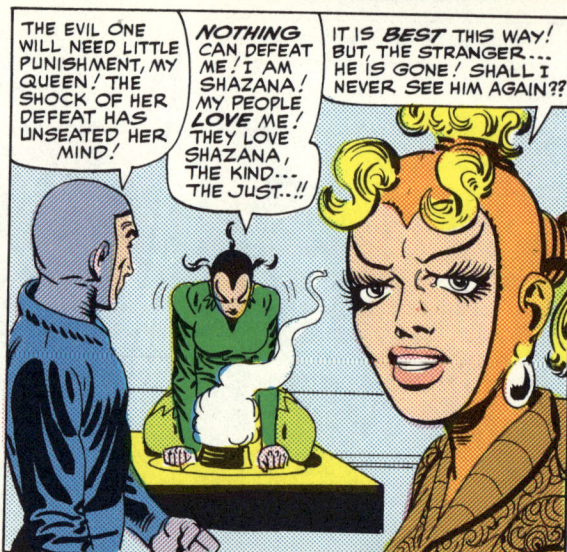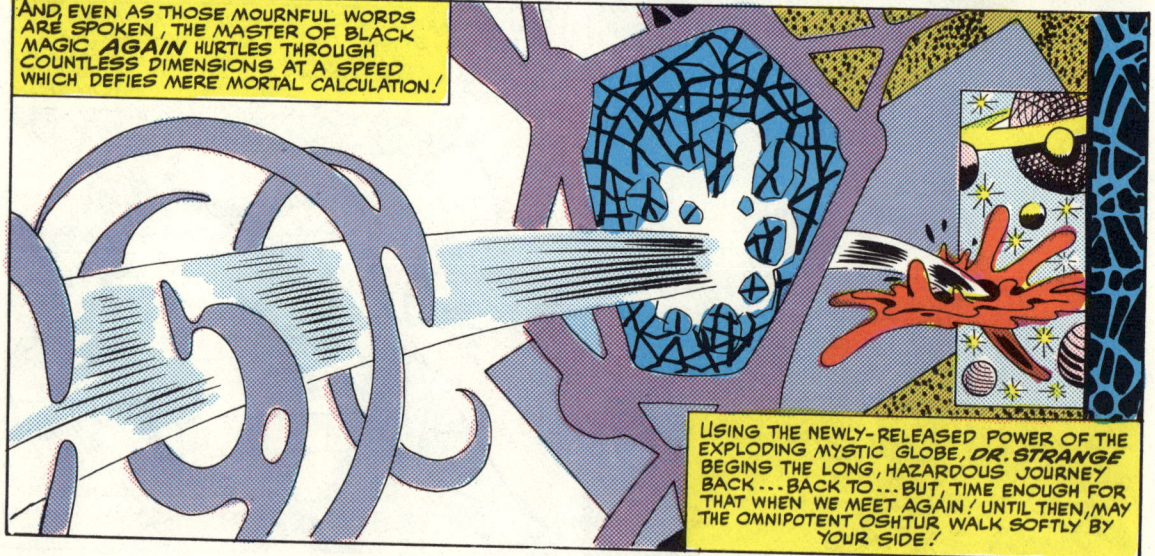

Here's a twist for you! The story that follows never appeared in a *Dr. Strange* magazine! It's not even a Dr. Strange story. It's a Spider-Man special! But, as Stevey Strange himself might say, "By the shades of the shadowy Seraphim, there's more to this than doth meet the eye!"

Actually, "The Wondrous World of Dr. Strange" is from the *Spider-Man Annual #2*. We wanted a yarn that would be really special, something that would verily rock our rabid readers. So, since ol' Steve Ditko was illustrating both Dr. Strange and Spidey at the time, it seemed like a natural to let Doc be the featured guest star in the web slinger's commemorative issue.

Then, to make it even more special, I figured it would be supersplendiferous to let Daring Ditko himself dream up the plot. Of course, I may have had a secondary little reason—like the fact that I didn't have the time to plot it myself and Samaritan Steve practically saved my life by handling that little chore. But that's nobody's business but ours, right?

Speaking of plotting, let me tell you here and now (which is one of the nuttiest phrases of all time—I certainly couldn't tell you there and then, could I? I mean, you can't *ever* be over there, 'cause wherever you are at a given time is always "here"! I hope you're all taking notes. There may be an exam!) Now where were we? Oh yes, I was gonna clue you in about our plotting. In case I never told you this before, Steve Ditko is one of the best plot men in the biz. When it comes to dreaming up story ideas, putting them together intricately, panel by panel, and utilizing the best of cinematic techniques, the guy's a whiz. Thus, the spectacular saga that is about to knock you out was basically concocted by our own Mr. D. But in case you're wondering what yours truly had to do with it . . .

Somebody has to put in the words. Lamentable as it may seem, they simply don't appear by magic. So, that's my job. After Steve did the hard part—after he dreamed up the story and illustrated it in his own unique style—I then got to do the fun part. I wrote all the squiggly little words: the dialog balloons and captions, the soliloquies and the snide remarks, and all the little sound effects that drove Steve bonkers 'cause they cluttered up his artwork! Yep, that's how we did it, and I hope you dig the daffy result.

Of course, the thing I liked the very best was putting in the little unexpected wisecracks (at least, I hope they were unexpected) wherever and whenever I had the chance. And names! How I love making up names! It took me as long to come up with Xandu as it did to write the first six pages! And don't blame me if it sounds like something out of Kipling; I like to kipple with the best of 'em!

But, about the story. I've a hunch it's gonna knock you out when you see how Spidey and Doc cross paths and get involved in the same adventure, and I think their relationship and attitudes toward each other worked out exactly the way you would have wanted. If I'm right, I know you'll be impressed. If I'm, wrong, don't tell me—you wouldn't wanna damage my ego!

But enough pointless prattle. One of the most memorable stories of all is waiting on the pages ahead—and you know how impatient us sorcerers get!

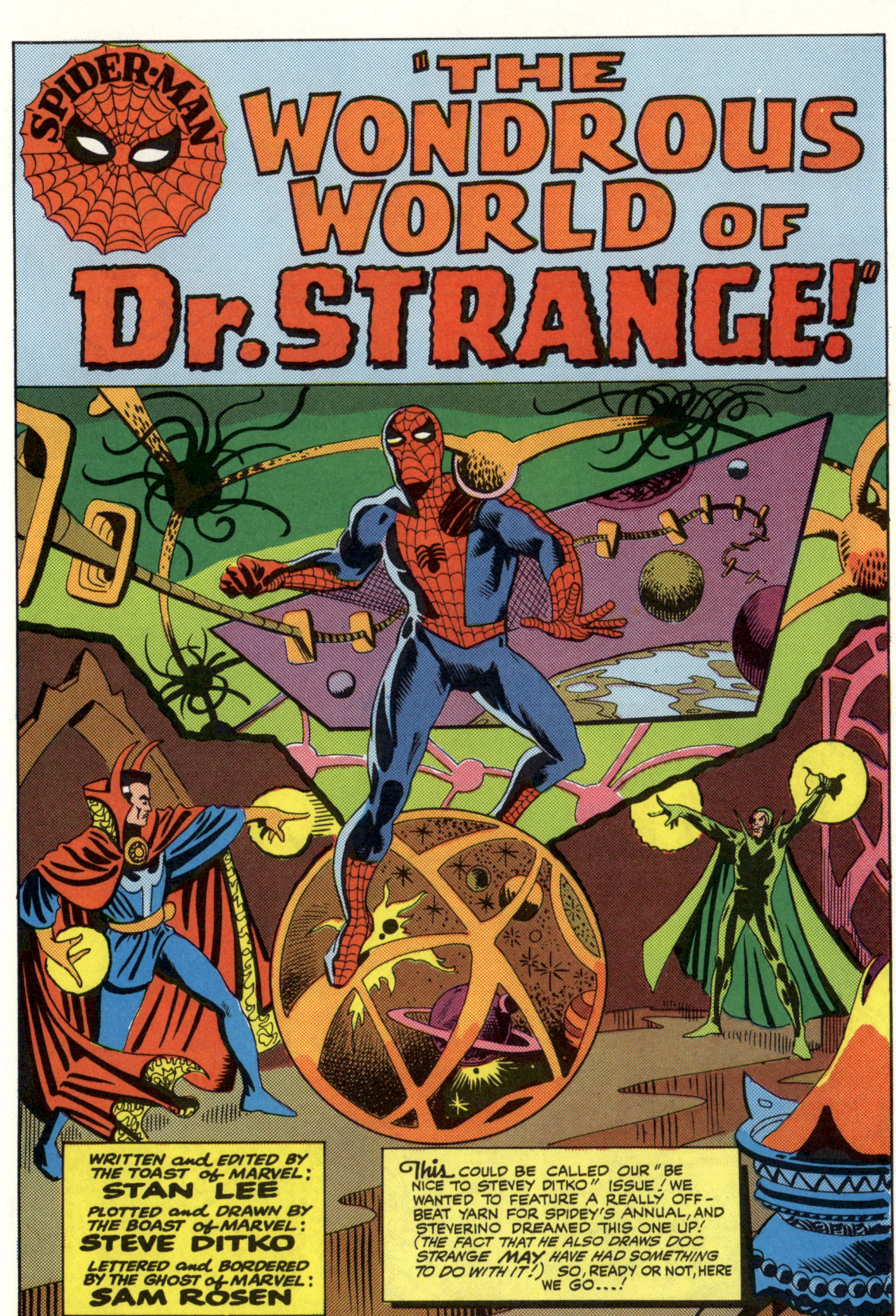

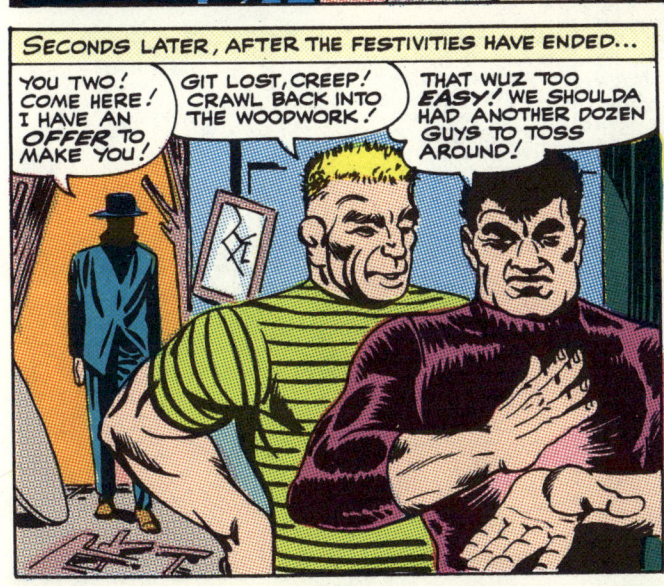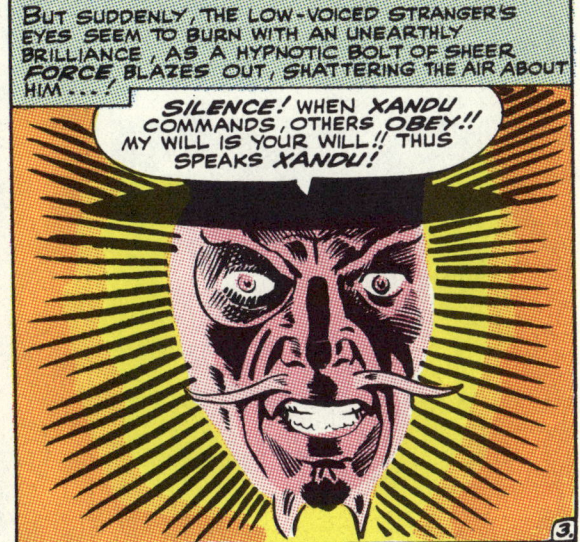

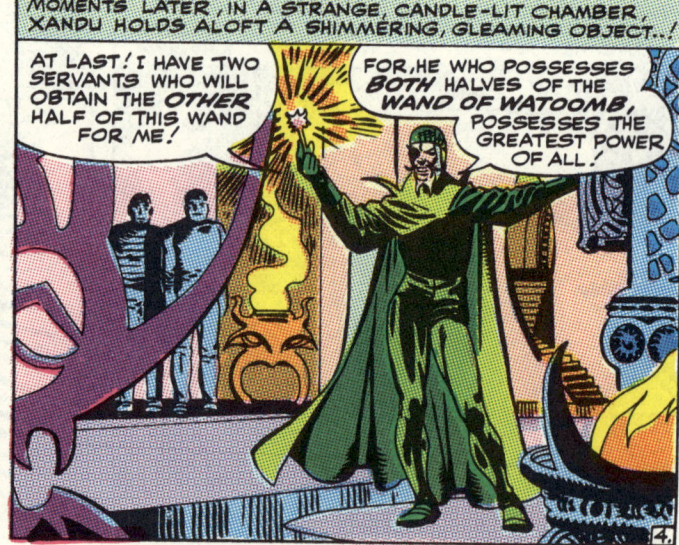

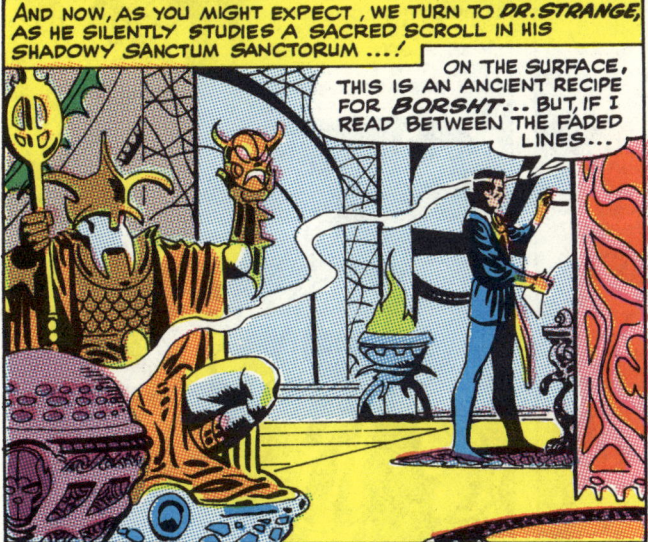

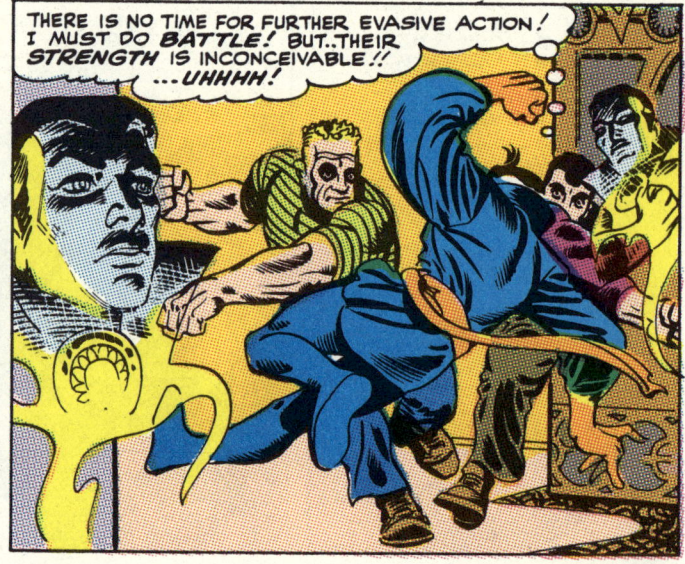
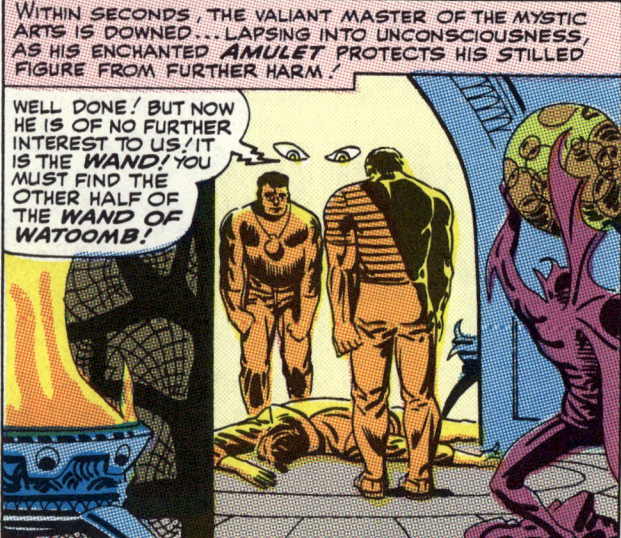

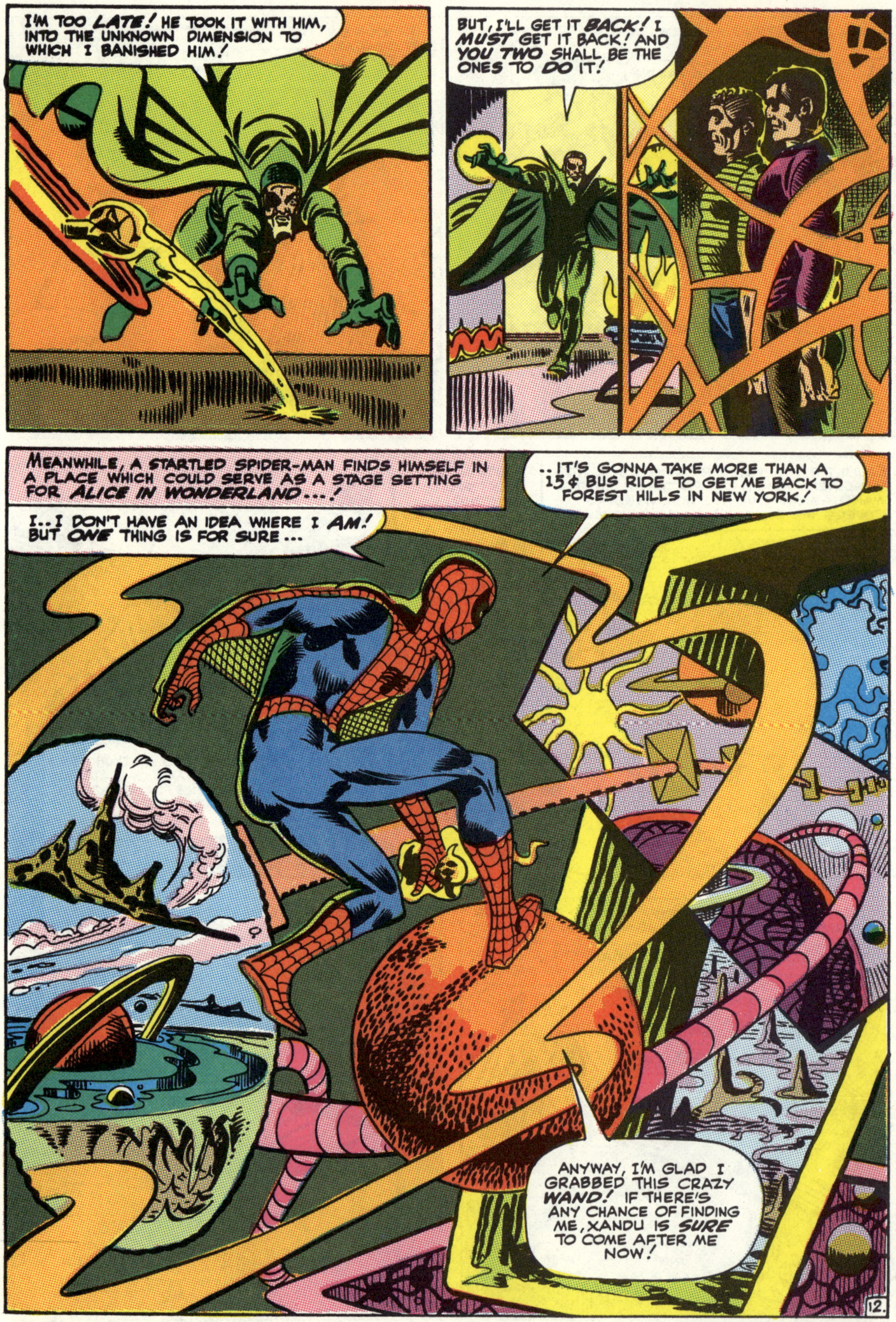

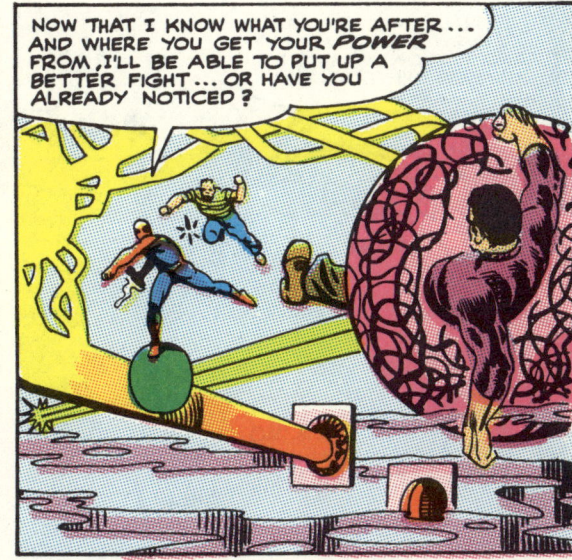

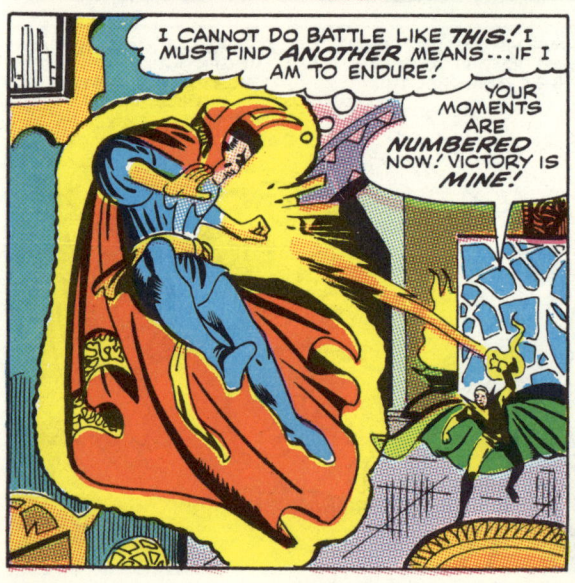

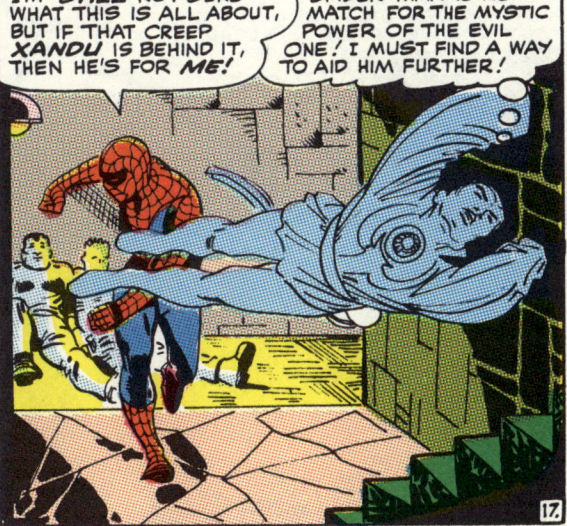

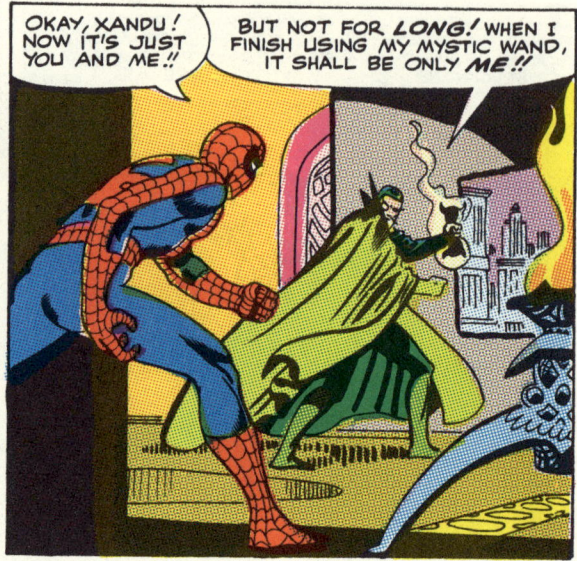

And now, are you really ready for this?

The following saga, which is perhaps one of the great contemporary classics of modern comicdom (if I do say so myself, despite my shyness), is especially notable for two reasons—reasons known only to those who are privy to the most closely guarded secrets in the hallowed halls of Marvel.

REASON #1: It marks the very last Dr. Strange story that I ever wrote. As a matter of fact, I had already stopped writing the awesome adventures of our peerless prestidigitator a few years earlier, but for some reason, I very much wanted to script this particular yarn. And so, I once again took typewriter in hand for my final fling with Stephen Strange at this time—and the reason was . . .

REASON #2: Barry Smith had been wanting to do this particular story for a long, long time. And I had wanted to do one last collaboration with Barry for an equally long time. So here's where we both got our chance.

You may remember the spectacular Mr. Smith as the artist who first helped us make *Conan the Barbarian* one of the comicbook triumphs of the seventies, under the script-writing and editing aegis of Roy Thomas. Well, Barry had always been a favorite illustrator of mine, and I just couldn't resist this chance to work with him on one of my all-time favorite strips.

As for the story itself, just between you and me, I'm crazy about it. Not only is the artwork indescribably beautiful, but the story is more than a mystical action adventure. It's an honest-to-Hoggoth, no-holds-barred, deep down, old-fashioned, no kiddin' *mystery*. And I've always grooved on mysteries!

Perhaps another reason it's one of my favorites is that Barry paced the story very slowly and somberly, giving me a chance to really write the type of dialogue I prefer for Dr. Strange. There was space enough to include a few of the inevitable incantations that I so truly love, as well as many opportunities for me to dig into the type of soul-searching commentary that is so important for a character like Stephen Strange. And wait until you learn which enemy our hero has to battle. But I won't tell you about it now—it's part of the many surprises you've got in store.

One suggestion. Since "While the World Spins Mad" is the final story in this volume, be sure to read it slowly. You see, as soon as you finish it, you'll be hit with another of my ubiquitous epilogues, and I'd like to spare you that for as long as possible.

Okay! We've savored and relished the world-famous artwork of Steve Ditko on the preceding pages. Now for a brain-blasting change of pace, let's dip into the artistic vision of Barry Smith as he portrays our supersorcerer in his own dazzling style.

Of course, while you're eagerly turning the page, I won't mind at all if I hear you enthusiastically whisper, "Make Mine Marvel!"

Dr. STRANGE MASTER OF THE MYSTIC ARTS!

WHILE THE WORLD SPINS MAD!

SPELLBINDING SCENARIO BY: STAN LEE
PHANTASMAGORIC PLOT & PENCILLING BY: BARRY SMITH
EMBELLISHMENT BY: DAN ADKINS
LETTERING BY: JOHN COSTANZA

107

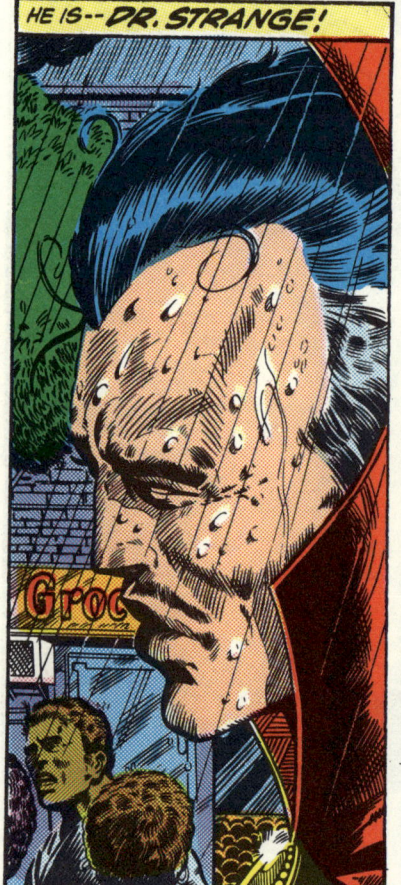

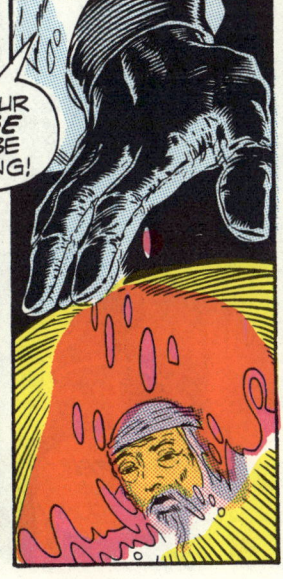

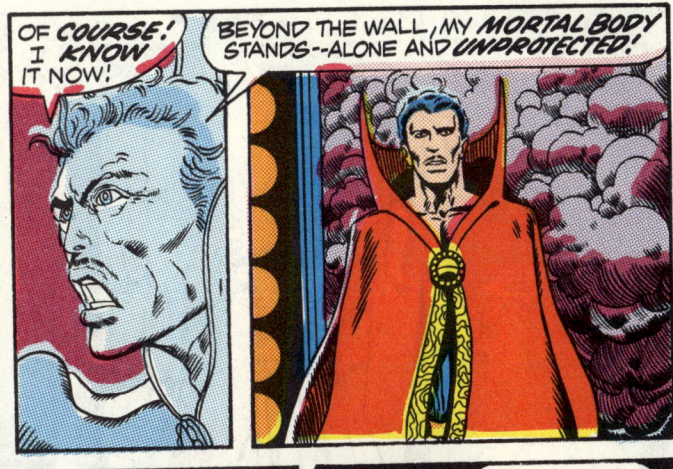

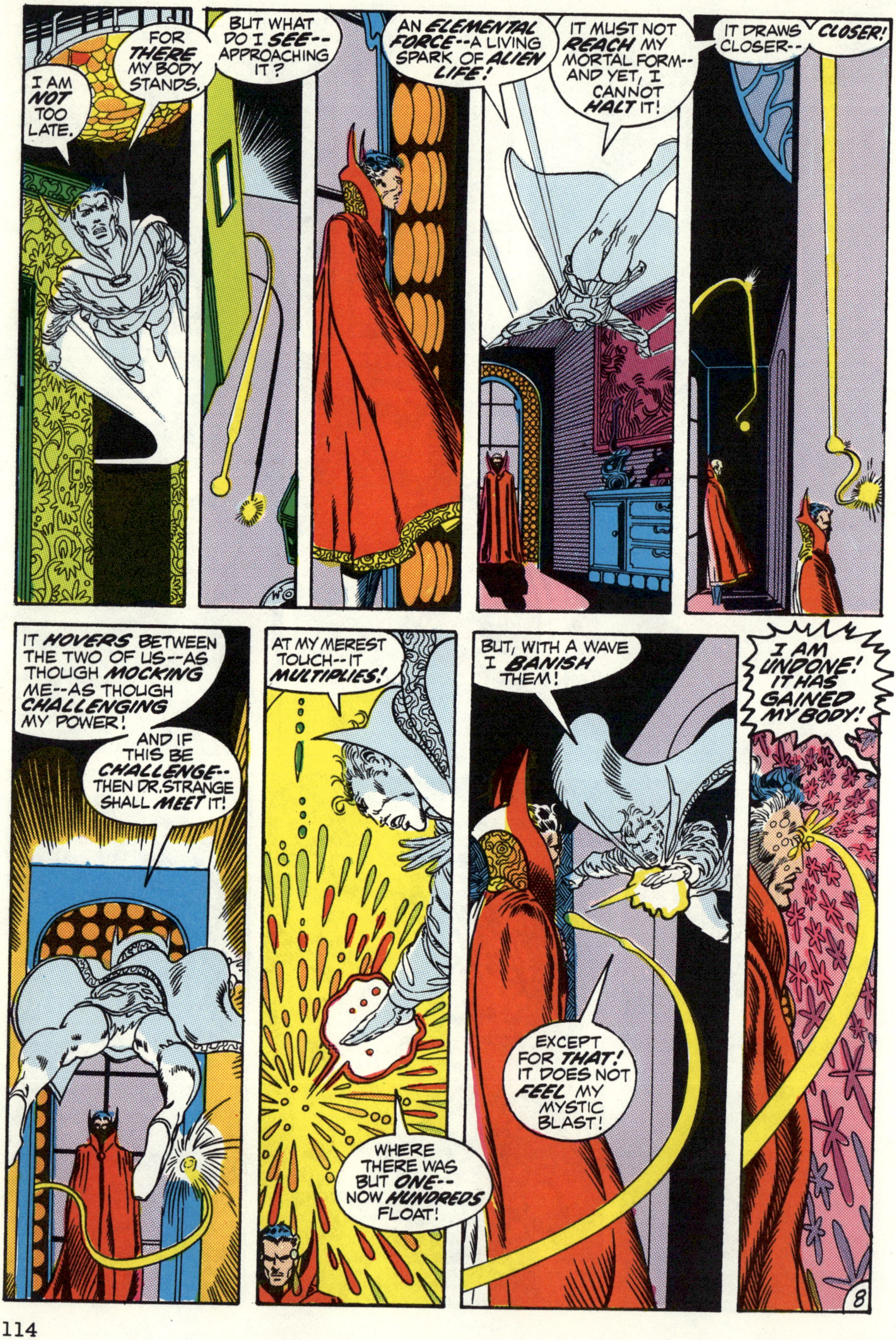

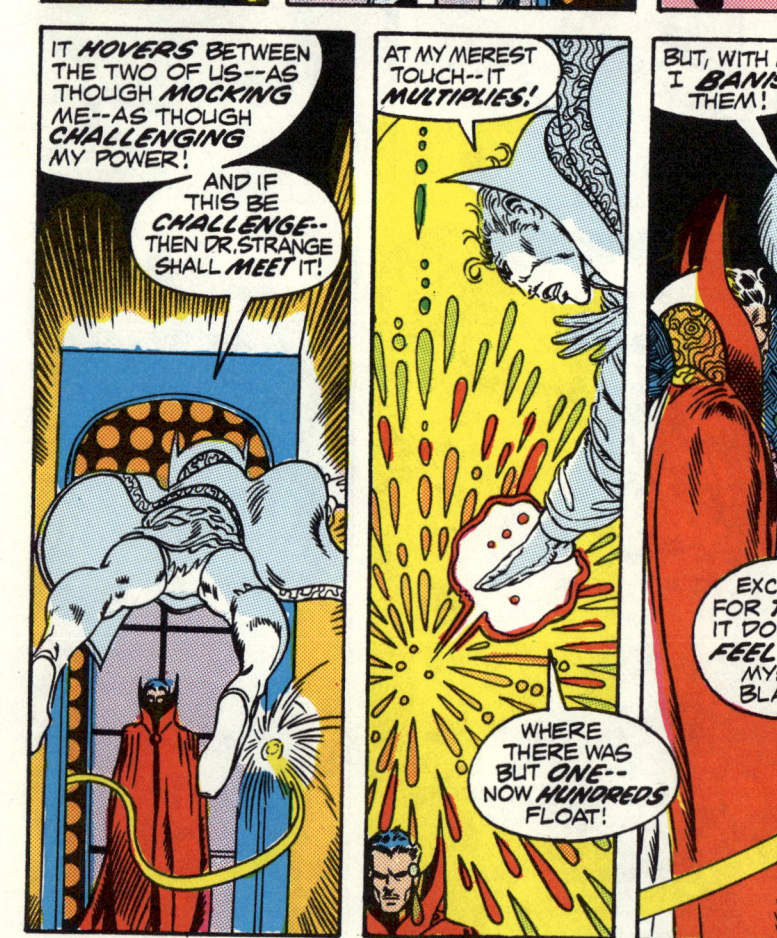

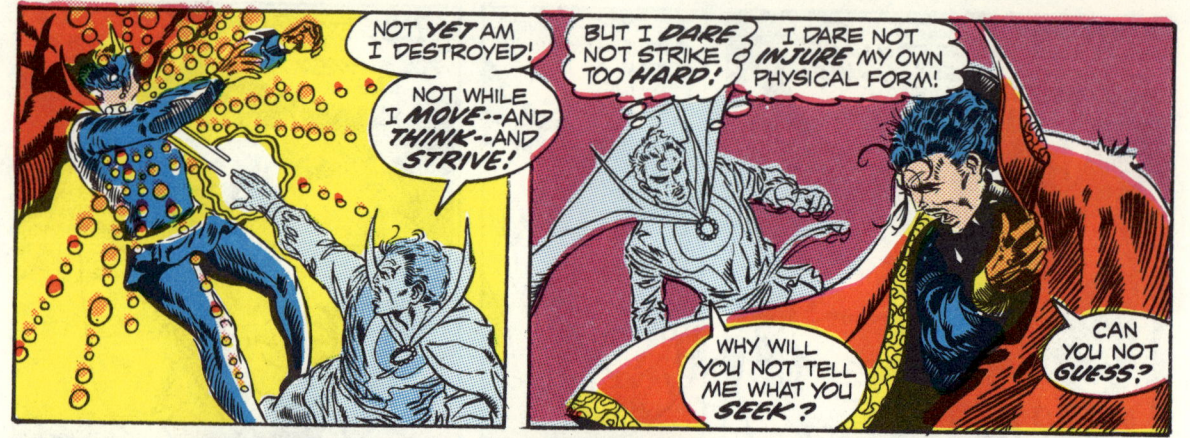

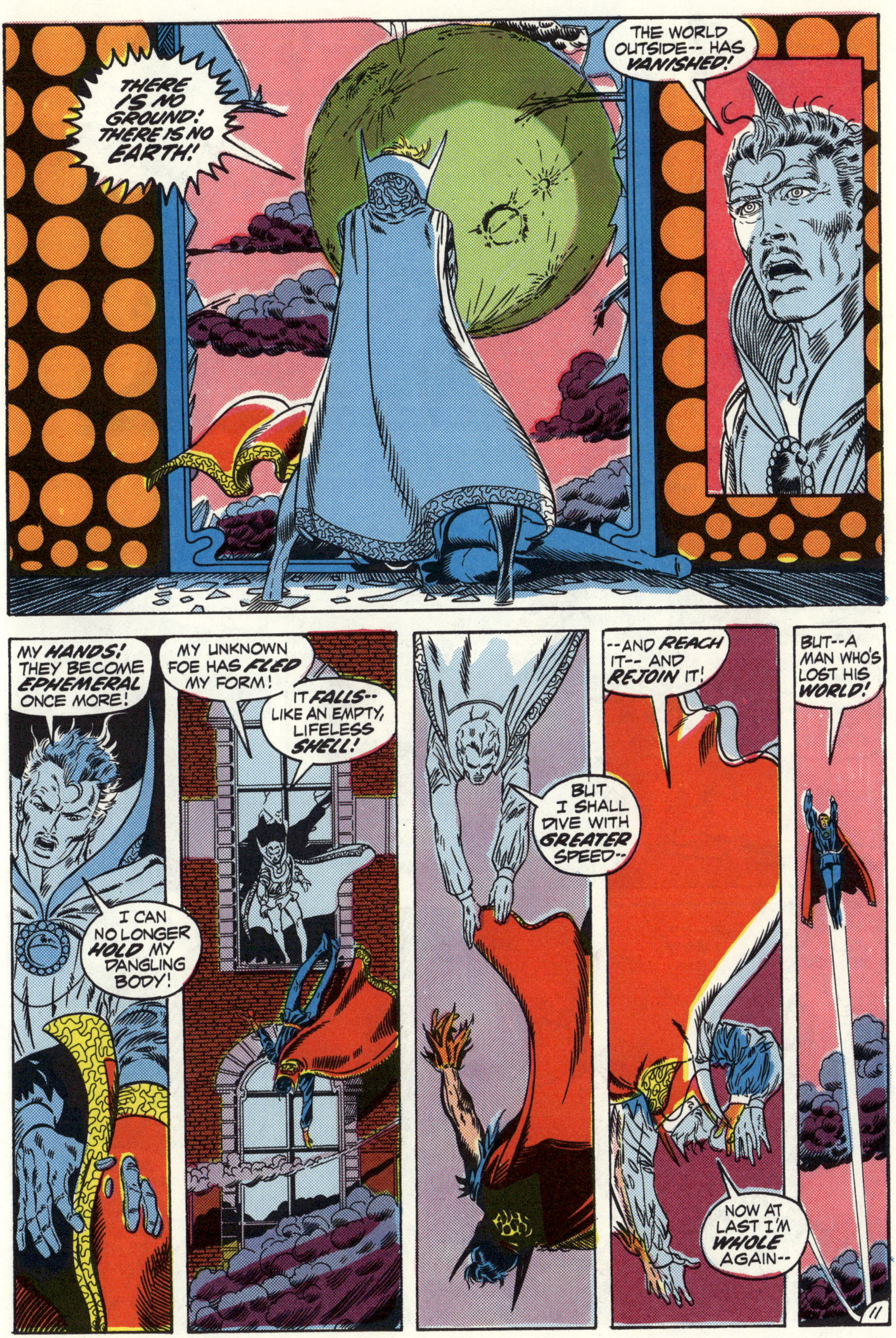

"THERE IS NO GROUND! THERE IS NO EARTH!"

"THE WORLD OUTSIDE-- HAS VANISHED!"

"MY HANDS! THEY BECOME EPHEMERAL ONCE MORE!"

"I CAN NO LONGER HOLD MY DANGLING BODY!"

"MY UNKNOWN FOE HAS FLED MY FORM!"

"IT FALLS-- LIKE AN EMPTY, LIFELESS SHELL!"

"BUT I SHALL DIVE WITH GREATER SPEED--"

"--AND REACH IT-- AND REJOIN IT!"

"BUT-- A MAN WHO'S LOST HIS WORLD!"

"NOW AT LAST I'M WHOLE AGAIN--"

117

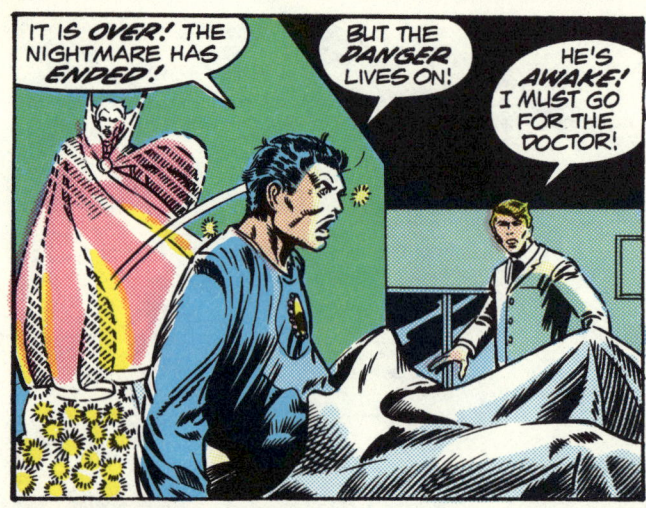

EPILOGUE

And there you have it—another magnificent milestone in Marvel's march to the mastery of myth and magic!

Or, as the world's greatest sorcerer might have so succinctly put it:

> In the name of
> the All-Seeing,
>
> In the name of
> the All-Sublime,
>
> In the name of
> the All-Freeing,
>
> We had to end this
> sometime!

Hope you had as much fun with our necromantical nonsense as we did, O Keeper of the Flame. And now, while we breathlessly wait for Volume Two, let's make sure we meet again, real soon, in the wonderful world of Marvel.

Till then, may thine amulet never rust nor thy cloak turn itself to dust! May thy days be bright and bathed in peace, and may thine ills and woes all cease!

Excelsior!

Stan